CW01652224

Cajun & Creole Cooking

CAROL BOWEN

•PARRAGON•

First published in Great Britain in 1994 by
Parragon Book Service Ltd
Unit 13–17
Avonbridge Trading Estate
Atlantic Road
Avonmouth
Bristol BS11 9QD

Copyright © 1994 Parragon Book Service Ltd

All rights reserved. No part of this publication may be reproduced, stored in a retrieval system or transmitted, in any form or by any means, electronic, mechanical, photocopying, recording or otherwise, without the prior permission of the copyright holder.

ISBN 1-85813-644-X (hbk)
ISBN 0-75251-292-7 (pbk)

Printed in Italy

Acknowledgements:
Design & DTP: Pedro & Frances Prá-Lopez/Kingfisher Design
Art Direction: Clive Hayball
Managing Editor: Alexa Stace
Special Photography: Martin Brigdale
Home Economist: Jill Eggleton
Step-by-step Photography: Karl Adamson
Step-by-step Home Economist: Joanna Craig
Styling: Helen Trent

Photographs on pages 6, 16, 28, 52 and 62 reproduced by permission of ZEFA Picture Library UK Ltd.

Note:
Cup measurements in this book are for American cups. Tablespoons are assumed to be 15 ml. Unless otherwise stated, milk is assumed to be full-fat, eggs are standard size 2 and pepper is freshly ground black pepper.

Contents

NATCHEZ

CHAPTER ONE

Starters

Hot, bubbling broths, laden with fish, shellfish, vegetables and just a hint of meat or poultry, are characteristic of Cajun appetizers. They come either hot and filling like Cajun Bean Soup or Louisiana Seafood Gumbo, to satisfy man-sized appetites; or light and spicy, like Eggs Sardou, to tempt the palate.

Many are Cajun: gutsy, rustic numbers made with the plentiful local ingredients which include time, patience and tender loving care; others reflect the more sophisticated Creole style, where specialities are conjured up by world-class chefs using the finest of fresh foods, and where presentation is all-important.

Both cooking styles and the dishes they produce reflect the gastronomic excellence in Louisiana, made possible by the variety of foodstuffs available. The diverse culinary tastes of the French, African, Spanish, Native Americans and Acadians who made up the area's population have been modified, but not entirely lost, coming together to create a cuisine that is unique and incomparable.

Opposite: *A traditional steamboat on the Mississippi at New Orleans, Louisiana.*

STEP 1

STEP 2

STEP 3

STEP 4

CAJUN BEAN SOUP

A hearty and wholesome soup made with colourful vegetables and nutritious butter beans – perfect for serving on cold wintry days.

SERVES 6

2 tbsp vegetable oil
125 g/4 oz streaky bacon, rinded and chopped
1 large onion, chopped
1 red (bell) pepper, cored, seeded and chopped
5 celery sticks, chopped
1 x 425 g/14 oz can chopped tomatoes
600 ml/1 pint/2½ cups vegetable stock
2 bay leaves
½ tsp Tabasco
1 tsp salt
2 x 475 g/15 oz cans butter beans, drained
chopped parsley, to garnish

1 Heat the oil in a large, heavy-based pan. Add the bacon and cook quickly until crisp.

2 Add the onion, (bell) pepper and celery and cook until just beginning to turn golden.

3 Add the chopped tomatoes, stock, bay leaves, Tabasco and salt, mixing well. Bring to the boil, reduce the heat and cook for 10 minutes.

4 Add the butter beans, stir well, cover and simmer for about 30 minutes, stirring occasionally, until the vegetables are tender.

5 Remove and discard the bay leaves. Serve the soup, ladled into warm soup bowls, sprinkled with parsley.

VARIATION

This soup could be made with other varieties of canned beans – black-eyed beans, cannellini beans, borlotti beans or red kidney beans. Some canned beans contain brine – rinse before using.

LOUISIANA SEAFOOD GUMBO

Gumbo is a hearty, thick soup, almost a stew. This New Orleans classic must be served with a scoop of hot, fluffy, cooked rice.

SERVES 4

1 tbsp plain flour
1 tsp paprika
350 g/12 oz monkfish fillets, cut into chunks
2 tbsp olive oil
1 onion, chopped
1 green (bell) pepper, cored, seeded and chopped
3 celery sticks, finely chopped
2 garlic cloves, crushed
175 g/6 oz okra, sliced
600 ml/1 pint/2½ cups vegetable stock
1 x 425 g/14 oz can chopped tomatoes
1 bouquet garni
125 g/4 oz peeled prawns (shrimp)
juice of 1 lemon
dash of Tabasco
2 tsp Worcestershire sauce
175 g/6 oz/generous 1 cup cooked long-grain American rice

1 Mix the flour with the paprika. Add the monkfish chunks and toss to coat well.

2 Heat the olive oil in a large, heavy-based pan. Add the monkfish pieces and fry until browned on all sides. Remove from the pan with a slotted spoon and set aside.

3 Add the onion, green (bell) pepper, celery, garlic and okra and fry gently for 5 minutes until softened.

4 Add the stock, tomatoes and bouquet garni. Bring to the boil, reduce the heat and simmer for 15 minutes.

5 Return the monkfish to the pan with the prawns (shrimp), lemon juice, Tabasco and Worcestershire sauces. Simmer for a further 5 minutes.

6 To serve, place a mound of cooked rice in each warmed, serving bowl, then ladle over the seafood gumbo.

VARIATION

In the South filé powder is used to flavour and thicken the gumbo. Filé powder is made from sassafras leaves and is very hard to find outside the US.

STEP 2

STEP 3

STEP 4

STEP 5

STEP 1

STEP 2

STEP 3

STEP 4

EGGS SARDOU

Eggs Sardou were created by Antoine's restaurant in New Orleans in honour of the French playwright, Victorien Sardou. They are perfect to serve for a late breakfast or brunch.

SERVES 4

2 warm muffins
4 canned or cooked artichoke hearts, heated until warm
8 anchovy fillets
4 eggs

HOLLANDAISE SAUCE:
150 g/5 oz/²/₃ cup butter
1 tbsp white wine vinegar
1 tbsp lemon juice
3 large egg yolks
¼ tsp caster sugar
¼ tsp salt
pinch of white pepper

1 To make the sauce, melt the butter in a pan and skim off the white foam that collects on top.

2 Heat the vinegar and lemon juice separately in small pans.

3 Put the egg yolks in a blender goblet with the sugar, salt, hot vinegar and hot lemon juice. Cover and blend for 5-6 seconds. Remove the lid, set the blender to maximum speed, then add the butter in a steady slow stream. The sauce will thicken and emulsify in about 45 seconds. Season with pepper to taste.

4 Split the muffins in half and place each half on a warmed serving plate. Top with a warm artichoke heart.

5 Arrange two anchovy fillets in a cross over the top of each artichoke heart on the muffins.

6 Poach the eggs in water until just cooked then place on top of each prepared muffin. Spoon or pour over the warm Hollandaise sauce and serve immediately.

VARIATION

The anchovy fillets can be replaced with anchovy paste (such as Gentleman's Relish) if liked. Spread over the muffins before topping with the artichoke hearts.

STEP 1

STEP 2

STEP 3

STEP 4

BAKED CRAB SHELLS

Crab is cooked with the "holy trinity" of vegetables – onion, green (bell) pepper and celery – sprinkled with breadcrumbs and baked until golden. Delicious as a special starter or light lunch dish.

SERVES 4
OVEN: 200°C/400°F/GAS 6

60 g/2 oz/¼ cup butter
2 garlic cloves, crushed
1 small onion, chopped
1 celery stick, finely chopped
½ green (bell) pepper, cored, seeded and chopped
½ red (bell) pepper, cored, seeded and chopped
½ fresh chilli, seeded and finely chopped
½ tsp chopped fresh thyme
150 ml/¼ pint/⅔ cup double (heavy) cream
salt and pepper
500 g/1 lb fresh or frozen crab meat, defrosted if frozen, flaked
60 g/2 oz/1 cup fresh breadcrumbs
celery leaves, to garnish

1 Melt the butter in a large, heavy-based frying pan. Add the garlic, onion, celery, green and red (bell) peppers, and chilli. Stir-fry for about 5 minutes, or until softened.

2 Add the thyme, cream and salt and pepper to taste, stirring constantly. Reduce the heat and simmer gently for about 4-5 minutes until slightly thickened.

3 Add the crab meat with half of the breadcrumbs, increase the heat and cook for about 1-2 minutes.

4 Remove from the heat and spoon into 4 scrubbed and oiled crab shells, ramekins or small gratin dishes and level the surfaces.

5 Sprinkle the remaining breadcrumbs over the tops then bake in the preheated oven for about 15 minutes until crisp and golden. Garnish with celery to serve.

ALTERNATIVE

The cream in the recipe could be replaced with a condensed soup such as chicken, prawn (shrimp) bisque or celery. Use 150 ml/¼ pint/⅔ cup undiluted soup.

CHAPTER TWO

Fish

Early Cajun settlers quickly learnt how to live off the land – and from the rivers and bayous of Louisiana. Trappers and fishermen often returned home laden with their catch and cooked it in big black pots over open wood fires. Maybe it is because of this legacy, or because there is such an abundance of seafood to be found in the state: gulf trout, pampano, redfish, snapper, catfish, crab, crawfish and oysters, that Cajun-Creole cuisine is so rich in imaginative seafood recipes.

Many fish and shellfish are cooked plain, coated in breadcrumbs or a batter and deep-fried, but almost invariably they are then given the full New Orleans treatment with a zippy, spicy sauce for pouring over or for dipping into. Many classics have that unmistakeable French touch by being baked *au gratin* or in a soufflé; others are a melting pot of French, Spanish and Black American influences, like Louisiana Seafood Paella and Rice and Shrimp Casserole; while yet others, notably Blackened Cajun Fish, are truly original and have become new classics of the American kitchen. The latter makes wonderful barbecue food – perfect for eating outdoors in the spirit of the old settlers.

Opposite: *A typical bayou in the swamps of Louisiana.*

STEP 1

STEP 2

STEP 3

STEP 4

LOUISIANA SEAFOOD PAELLA

A classic Deep South dish perfect for a special occasion.

SERVES 4

2 tbsp vegetable oil
1 green (bell) pepper, cored, seeded and chopped
1 onion, chopped
1 celery stick, chopped
1/2 tsp dried thyme
Creole Sauce (see page 41)
150 ml/1/4 pt/2/3 cup fish stock or water
75 ml/3 fl oz/5 tbsp double (heavy) cream
300 g/10 oz/scant 2 cups cooked long-grain rice
250 g/8 oz peeled prawns (shrimp)
125 g/4 oz cooked mussels
175 g/6 oz crab meat
2 tbsp snipped chives or spring onion (scallion) tops
salt
wedges of lime, to garnish

1 Heat the oil in a large heavy-based pan. Add the (bell) pepper, onion and celery and fry gently for 10 minutes until soft but not brown.

2 Stir in the thyme, Creole sauce and stock or water and simmer for 5 minutes over gentle heat.

3 Add the cream and mix well to blend. Simmer for 5 minutes.

4 Add the rice, prawns (shrimp), mussels, crab meat, chives and salt to taste. Stir in carefully so that the crab meat remains in chunky pieces. Cook for 2-3 minutes until hot.

5 Turn on to a warmed serving dish and garnish with wedges of lime to serve. Serve immediately.

FISH STOCK

You can make your own fish stock by simmering fish heads, bones and trimmings in water for 15-20 minutes. Do not cook for longer or the stock will be bitter. Freeze any surplus stock – it is very useful for fish soups and chowders.

BLACKENED CAJUN FISH

"Blackened" is not a traditional Cajun cooking technique but one invented by the famous New Orleans chef, Paul Prudhomme.

STEP 2

STEP 3

STEP 4

STEP 5

SERVES 4

4 fish fillets (red fish or bass for example), cut about 1 cm/½ in thick
60 g/2 oz/¼ cup butter, melted

CAJUN SPICE MIXTURE:
1 tbsp salt
2 tsp garlic powder
2 tsp ground black pepper
1½ tsp ground cumin
½-1 tsp cayenne pepper (to taste)
1½ tsp paprika
1½ tsp barbecue seasoning powder
boiled rice with spicy butter dressing, to serve (see variation, below)

1 Blend the ingredients for the spice mixture together.

2 Dip the fish fillets in the melted butter then sprinkle each side evenly with the seasoning mixture.

3 Meanwhile, put a heavy-based cast iron frying pan on to heat slowly and steadily until very hot indeed. Don't heat too fast – the heat needs to be steady and even. Hold the palm of your hand just above the surface of the pan – the pan will be hot enough when you can feel a strong rising heat.

4 Press the fish fillets down firmly on to the very hot surface with a fish slice. There should be an almighty hiss and a great deal of smoke and steam. Cook for 1-2 minutes until blackened on one side.

5 Turn the fish over, using the slice, and cook the other side. The surface should be well charred on both sides when cooked.

6 Serve hot, with any remaining melted butter poured over, and with cooked rice.

VARIATION

Blackened fish is delicious served with rice tossed in a red chilli and coriander hot butter dressing. Melt 60 g/2 oz/¼ cup butter in a pan, add 1-2 sliced red chillies, 2 teaspoons cumin or poppy seeds and fry for 1 minute. Stir in a squeeze of lemon juice, cooked rice and 2 tablespoons chopped mixed parsley and coriander. Stir well into the hot rice and serve.

AUBERGINE (EGGPLANT) PIROGUES

A pirogue is a type of canoe used in the bayous for fishing and travelling in the southern part of Louisiana. Aubergines (eggplant) hollowed out and filled with a fishy mixture resemble these longboats.

SERVES 4
OVEN: 200°C/400°F/GAS 6

2 large aubergines (eggplant)
60 g/2 oz/¼ cup butter
1 large onion, chopped
1 green (bell) pepper, cored, seeded and chopped
1 celery stick, finely chopped
175 g/6 oz peeled prawns (shrimp)
90 g/3 oz button mushrooms, chopped
60 g/2 oz/1 cup soft white breadcrumbs
salt and cayenne pepper
125 g/4 oz/1 cup Cheddar, grated (optional)

1 Halve the aubergines (eggplant) and cut out the centres, leaving a 1 cm/½ in thick shell. Chop the flesh coarsely and set aside.

2 Cook the aubergines (eggplant) halves in boiling salted water for about 5 minutes, then drain thoroughly.

3 Meanwhile, melt the butter in a pan, add the onion, green (bell) pepper and celery until softened. Add the chopped aubergine (eggplant) flesh and cook until golden. Add the prawns (shrimp) and mushrooms and cook for a further 3-4 minutes.

4 Remove the vegetable mixture from the heat and stir in the breadcrumbs. Season with salt and cayenne pepper to taste. Pile into the aubergine (eggplant) halves and sprinkle with the cheese, if using.

5 Arrange the aubergine (eggplant) halves in an ovenproof dish and bake in the preheated oven for 20-25 minutes until golden and bubbly. Serve hot with a crisp seasonal salad.

VARIATION

This mixture is often used to stuff mirlitons in Cajun cooking. Mirlitons are mild-flavoured members of the squash family that have a pear shape. They can be found in good supermarkets and are well worth trying. To use instead of aubergines (eggplant), boil 4 whole mirlitons in boiling salted water for about 45 minutes until tender. Drain, cool and halve lengthwise. Gently remove the seeds, scoop out the flesh to leave a shell and chop the flesh. Use the flesh instead of the aubergine (eggplant) flesh and fill the halved shells in the same way. Bake for about 15-20 minutes.

STEP 1

STEP 2

STEP 3

STEP 4

STEP 1

STEP 2

STEP 3

STEP 5

CRAYFISH PIES

If crayfish are unavailable use peeled tiger prawns (shrimp), cut into bite-sized pieces.

SERVES 4
OVEN: 200°C/400°F/GAS 6

PASTRY:
175 g/6 oz/1½ cups plain flour
pinch of salt
90 g/3 oz/6 tbsp butter
1 egg yolk
3-4 tbsp cold water

FILLING:
2 tbsp vegetable oil
15 g/½ oz/2 tbsp plain flour
½ green (bell) pepper, cored, seeded and finely chopped
½ small onion, finely chopped
1 celery stick, finely chopped
250 ml/8 fl oz/1 cup double (heavy) cream
90 g/3 oz/6 tbsp unsalted butter
6 spring onions (scallions), finely chopped
1 garlic clove, crushed
350 g/12 oz peeled crayfish tails
1½-2 tsp Cajun Spice Mixture (see page 20)

1 To make the pastry, sift the flour with the salt, then rub in the butter until the mixture resembles fine breadcrumbs. Make a well in the centre and add the egg yolk with the water. Mix to a firm dough. Roll out the pastry thinly and use to line 4 x 10 cm/4 in fluted flan tins. Chill for 20 minutes then bake "blind" for 10 minutes. Remove the paper and beans and bake for a further 5 minutes until golden.

2 To make the filling, heat the oil until it begins to smoke. Stir in the flour and cook, stirring briskly, for about 2-3 minutes or until a dark-red/brown roux is formed.

3 Remove from the heat and immediately add the (bell) peppers, onion and celery. Stir briskly until the mixture cools.

4 Meanwhile, heat the cream to a simmer, gradually add to the roux mixture, bring to the boil and whisk to make a thickened sauce.

5 Heat the butter in a frying pan. Add the spring onions (scallions) and garlic and cook for 1 minute. Add the crayfish tails (reserving 4 for garnish) and the spice mixture. Sauté for about 3 minutes until hot and cooked through. Stir in the sauce and mix well.

6 Spoon the mixture into the tartlet cases, garnish with the reserved tails and serve at once.

STEP 1

STEP 3

STEP 4

STEP 5

LOUISIANA RICE & SHRIMP

Louisiana's capital is New Orleans, which boasts the best of excellent dining. Be it Cajun (country food) or Creole (smart city food), both cooking styles rely on locally grown rice and seafood.

SERVES 4

60 g/2 oz/¼ cup butter or margarine
4 celery sticks, finely chopped
1 large onion, chopped
1/2 green (bell) pepper, cored and chopped
1 x 295 g/10¾ oz can condensed cream of mushroom soup
150 ml/¼ pt/⅔ cup water
500 g/1 lb peeled crayfish tails or shrimps
2 tbsp chopped parsley
750 g/1½ lb/4¼ cups hot cooked American long-grain rice
cayenne and black pepper, to taste
shrimps and celery leaves, to garnish

1 Melt the butter or margarine in a large, heavy-based pan. Add the celery and cook until tender, but not brown, for about 10-15 minutes.

2 Add the onion and (bell) pepper and cook for a further 5 minutes.

3 Blend the soup with the water then stir into the vegetables.

4 Add the crayfish tails or shrimps and cook over a low heat for about 10 minutes, stirring frequently. Add the chopped parsley and cook for a further 5 minutes.

5 Stir in the cooked rice, season to taste with cayenne and black pepper and heat through for 2-3 minutes before serving.

CRAYFISH

Crayfish look like miniature lobsters – they are about 7-10 cm/3-4 in. A dark greeny-brown, they become deep red or bright pink when cooked and have a sweet, delicate flavour. They are found in freshwater lakes and streams in many parts of the US and Europe.

CLOTHESLINE
1125
PIN-STRIPE
PIN STRIPE
BRASS BAND
NEW ORLEANS, LA.

CHAPTER THREE

Meat & Poultry

Long-simmered, tender and spicy one-pot meals such as gumbos, jambalayas and vegetable stews with spicy, coarse-textured sausages make the most of succulent beef, tasty pork and flavoursome chicken in this chapter. These are recipes served strictly Southern style where there is always something bubbling on the back burner or gently simmering to the steady beat of soul music. No wonder legend holds that "the good and righteous in Louisiana don't go to heaven, but to the big kitchen in the sky. Glory, Halleluyah!"

It isn't just the careful and inspired preparation of these dishes that makes them such a success: it's also the piquant choice of French sauces, Spanish spices, country seasonings and soul food herbs, judiciously, if not sparingly, used in their makeup.

Undoubtedly their continued success and longevity is assured down the centuries because they are meals that were always intended to be shared by one and all, be it feast or famine in the Deep South. Such dishes make superb party food . Entertaining is seemingly effortless when a huge potful can be made well ahead, kept warm without spoiling for hours, and can be eked out with a little extra rice or cornbread should unexpected guests arrive or when party numbers swell, as in a traditional Fais Do Do!

Opposite: *A brass band entertains passersby on the streets of New Orleans.*

BATON ROUGE CHICKEN GUMBO

Everyone in the state of Louisiana has their own favourite gumbo recipe. This one uses chicken with prawns (shrimp), okra and a little belly of pork: a recipe that is hard to improve upon.

SERVES 4-6

30 g/ 1 oz/ 2 tbsp butter
1 tbsp corn oil
30 g/ 1 oz/ 1/4 cup plain flour
90 g/ 3 oz belly of pork, sliced
1 large onion, sliced
2 celery sticks, chopped
500 g/ 1 lb okra, trimmed and sliced
1 x 425 g/ 14 oz can peeled tomatoes
2 garlic cloves, crushed
1 litre/ 1 3/4 pints/ 4 1/2 cups chicken stock or water
250 g/ 8 oz peeled prawns (shrimp)
500 g/ 1 lb cooked chicken, skinned and cut into bite-sized pieces
1 tsp Tabasco
500 g/ 1 lb/ 3 cups hot cooked rice, to serve

1 Heat the butter and oil in a small, heavy-based pan. Add the flour and cook, stirring frequently, over a low heat until the roux turns a rich brown colour (but be careful not to burn or it will taste bitter). Set aside.

2 Meanwhile, in a large pan, sauté the pork slices, without extra fat, until they are golden brown on all sides and the fat has been rendered. Add the sliced onion and celery and cook for a further 5 minutes.

3 Stir in the okra and sauté for a further 3 minutes. Stir in the tomatoes and garlic and simmer over gentle heat for 15 minutes.

4 Gradually add the stock to the browned roux, mixing and blending well, then add to the okra mixture. Cover and simmer for 1 hour.

5 Add the prawns (shrimp) and chicken to the okra mixture, cook for a further 5 minutes, then stir in the Tabasco.

6 Spoon the gumbo into individual serving bowls and top with a scoop of hot cooked rice.

GUMBO

Gumbo is a characteristic Creole dish, with its hint of Spanish, African and Native American flavours. Its name derives from the Bantu word for okra, an essential ingredient.

STEP 1

STEP 2

STEP 3

STEP 5

STEP 1

STEP 2

STEP 3

STEP 4

JAMBALAYA

Jambalaya, New Orlean's paella, dates back to the 18th century, when it was served as slave food. Today, this hearty rice dish can contain any number of meats, such as chicken, duck, ham or sausage.

SERVES 4

60 g/2 oz/¼ cup butter
2 onions, chopped
2 garlic cloves, crushed
5 celery sticks, chopped
1 red (bell) pepper, cored, seeded and chopped
1 green (bell) pepper, cored, seeded and chopped
1 tsp Cajun Spice Mixture (see page 20)
250 g/8 oz/1 cup long-grain rice
1 x 425 g/14 oz can tomatoes, drained and chopped
500 g/1 lb cooked assorted meats (chicken, duck, ham or sausage), sliced or diced
250 ml/8 fl oz/1 cup vegetable stock or white wine
1 tsp salt
parsley sprigs, to garnish

1 Melt the butter in a large, heavy-based pan. Add the onions, garlic, celery, (bell) peppers and spice mixture and mix well.

2 Add the rice and stir well to coat the grains in the butter mixture.

3 Add the tomatoes, diced meat, stock or wine and salt. Bring to the boil, stirring well.

4 Reduce the heat, cover and simmer for about 15 minutes or until the rice is cooked and fluffy and has absorbed all the liquid. If the mixture seems to be too dry then add a little boiling water, tablespoon by tablespoon, towards the end of the cooking time.

5 Serve the jamabalaya on warm plates, garnished with parsley.

SEAFOOD JAMBALAYA

Prepare and cook as above but use 500 g/ 1 lb assorted seafood, such as shrimps, prawns (shrimp), crab, lobster meat and cooked oysters.

STEP 1

STEP 3

STEP 4

STEP 5

CHICKEN ETOUFFE

Etouffé means smothered and is a popular way of presenting food in Cajun cuisine. Here, strips of chicken and vegetables are smothered in a thickened dark sauce flavoured with basil.

SERVES 4-6

60 g/2 oz/$\frac{1}{4}$ cup butter
1 small onion, chopped
1 small green (bell) pepper, cored, seeded and chopped
1 celery stick, chopped
1 red (bell) pepper, cored, seeded and chopped
1 small red chilli, seeded and finely chopped
1 tsp Cajun Spice Mixture (see page 20)
1 tsp chopped fresh basil
salt
2 tbsp vegetable oil
2 tbsp flour
475 ml/16 fl oz/2 cups rich chicken stock
500 g/1 lb skinless, boned chicken breasts, cut into strips or bite-sized pieces
4 spring onions (scallions), chopped

1 Melt the butter in a large, heavy-based pan. Add the onion, green (bell) pepper, celery, red (bell) pepper and chilli and cook over gentle heat until softened, about 5 minutes.

2 Add the Cajun Spice Mixture, basil and salt to taste and cook for a further 2 minutes.

3 Meanwhile, heat the oil in a pan, add the flour and cook, slowly, until a rich red/brown roux is formed, whisk constantly to prevent the roux from scorching and becoming bitter.

4 Gradually add the stock and whisk well to make a smooth thickened sauce. Pour the sauce over the vegetable mixture and allow to simmer for about 15 minutes.

5 Add the chicken strips and the spring onions (scallions) and cook for a further 10 minutes, stirring occasionally until the chicken is cooked and tender.

6 Serve with cooked long-grain rice or freshly cooked fluffy couscous.

COUSCOUS

Quick-cooking couscous is now available. To prepare, simply pour on boiling water to cover, leave to absorb, then fluff up with a fork (follow the instructions on the packet).

GRILLADES (WITH GRITS)

Grillades is a meat and vegetable stew in a thick gravy. It is considered to be Bayou breakfast food and would always be served with grits, a kind of creamy cereal (not unlike porridge) made from corn.

SERVES 6

4 tbsp olive oil
1 kg/2 lb veal fillet, pork tenderloin or turkey breast, cut into 7 x 10 cm/3 x 4 in strips
60 g/2 oz/½ cup plain flour
3 onions, chopped
2 green (bell) peppers, cored, seeded and chopped
4 celery sticks, finely chopped
1 garlic clove, crushed
500 g/1 lb ripe tomatoes, skinned, seeded and chopped
2 tbsp tomato purée (paste)
1 tsp chopped fresh thyme
½-1 tsp Tabasco
1½ tsp paprika
¼ tsp cayenne pepper
1 tsp salt
150 ml/¼ pint/⅔ cup vegetable stock
150 ml/¼ pint/⅔ cup white wine
grits, to serve (see right)

1 Heat the oil in a large, heavy-based pan. Add the meat strips and fry quickly on both sides until it changes colour. Remove with slotted spoon and set aside.

2 Add the flour to the pan juices and mix well. Cook over a gentle heat, stirring constantly, until the roux changes to a rich brown colour.

3 Add the onions, (bell) peppers, celery and garlic and mix well. Cover and cook over a gentle heat for about 15 minutes.

4 Return the meat to the pan with the tomatoes, tomato purée (paste), thyme, Tabasco, paprika, cayenne, salt, stock and wine, mixing well.

5 Cover and simmer gently for a further 40-45 minutes, or until the meat and vegetables are cooked and tender.

6 Serve hot with grits, if liked.

FOR THE GRITS

Place 600ml/1 pint/2½ cups milk, and water or stock in a pan. Add 165 g/5½ oz hominy grits (or 175 g/6 oz couscous) and bring to the boil, stirring constantly. Add 1 tablespoon butter and 1 teaspoon salt, partially cover and cook over a very gentle heat for 15 minutes.

STEP 1

STEP 2

STEP 3

STEP 4

STEP 1

STEP 3

STEP 5

STEP 6

LOUISIANA DUCK WITH BISCUITS

The "biscuits" in this dish are delicious scone-like rounds that sit on top of the savoury duck mixture, rather like a cobbler topping. In Louisiana these accompany many dishes containing chicken, fish or game.

SERVES 6
OVEN: 220°C/425°F/GAS 7

BISCUITS:
250 g/8 oz/2 cups self-raising flour
1/2 tsp Cajun Spice Mixture (see page 20)
125 g/4 oz/1/2 cup chilled butter
175 ml/6 fl oz/3/4 cup single cream

FILLING:
1 tbsp vegetable oil
1 tbsp plain flour
150ml/1/4 pint/2/3 cup chicken or duck stock
2 tbsp dry vermouth
30 g/1 oz/2 tbsp butter
500 g/1 lb cooked duck, cut into bite-sized pieces
2 rashers bacon, rinded and chopped
2 tbsp chopped red (bell) pepper
6 tbsp double (heavy) cream
3 spring onions (scallions), finely chopped
milk, to glaze

1 To make the biscuits, place the flour and spice mixture in a blender or food processor with the butter and process until it is finely mixed and resembles breadcrumbs. Add the cream and process again to make a soft dough. Form the dough into a ball, wrap in foil and chill in the refrigerator for 30 minutes.

2 Meanwhile, to make the filling, heat the oil in a pan, add the flour and cook gently for about 4-5 minutes to make a straw-coloured roux, stirring constantly. Gradually blend in the stock and vermouth to make a smooth sauce.

3 Heat the butter in a pan, add the duck, bacon and red pepper and cook until well coloured.

4 Stir in the sauce, cream and spring onions (scallions). Cook the mixture gently for about 2 minutes then pour into a shallow pie dish.

5 Roll out the dough to a thickness of about 1 cm/1/2 in, then stamp out about 18 rounds with a 5 cm/2 in scone cutter.

6 Prick the pastry rounds with a fork then arrange in overlapping rows over the duck mixture. Brush with milk to glaze then bake in the preheated oven for about 15 minutes until cooked and golden.

MARDI GRAS MEATBALLS

A colourful dish of meatballs in a gutsy tomato-based Creole sauce. You can also serve the sauce with meatloaf, sausages, chicken and pasta.

SERVES 6

MEATBALLS:
500 g/1 lb minced beef or pork
1 onion, chopped
60 g/2 oz/1 cup breadcrumbs
1 egg, beaten
salt and pepper
flour, to dust
2 tbsp vegetable oil
chopped parsley, to garnish
boiled rice or pasta, to serve

CREOLE SAUCE:
2 tbsp vegetable oil
1 onion, finely chopped
3 celery sticks, chopped
1 garlic clove, crushed
1 green (bell) pepper, cored, seeded and chopped
1 red (bell) pepper, cored, seeded and chopped
1 x 425 g/14 oz can chopped tomatoes
1 tsp molasses
1 tbsp lemon juice
pinch of ground bay leaves
Tabasco, to taste

1 To make the meatballs, mix the mince with the onion, breadcrumbs, egg and salt and pepper to taste. Divide and form into 24 meatballs, shaping them with your hands. Spread some flour on a flat plate and roll the meatballs in the flour to coat. Set aside.

2 To make the sauce, heat the oil in a pan, add the onion, celery, garlic and (bell) peppers and cook for about 10 minutes until softened.

3 Add the tomatoes, molasses, lemon juice, bay leaves, Tabasco and salt and pepper to taste. Bring to the boil, cover and simmer for 15 minutes.

4 Meanwhile, heat the oil in a large frying pan and fry the meatballs until brown on all sides.

5 Remove the meatballs from the pan with a slotted spoon and add to the sauce. Simmer gently for 20 minutes, then serve with rice or pasta. Sprinkle with chopped parsley to garnish.

MOLASSES

Molasses is a traditional ingredient in US cooking – it is a dark syrup left over when sugar cane is refined, with a strong, rich flavour.

STEP 1

STEP 2

STEP 3

STEP 4

CAJUN ROAST BEEF

Ring the changes for a special Sunday lunch or dinner party with these tasty ribs of beef stuffed fit to burst with a savoury breadcrumb mixture. Serve with a wine-flavoured sauce made from the pan juices.

SERVES 4
OVEN: 220°C/425°F/GAS 7

2 ribs of beef, each weighing about 950 g/ 1¾ lb, trimmed

STUFFING:
15 g/½ oz/1 tbsp butter
½ onion, chopped
½ small green (bell) pepper, cored, seeded and chopped
1 small celery stick, finely chopped
2 garlic cloves, crushed
1 tsp chopped fresh thyme
¼-½ tsp cayenne pepper (to taste)
60 g/2 oz/1 cup soft white breadcrumbs
2 bay leaves
salt and pepper
2 tbsp olive oil
1 tbsp flour
175 ml/6 fl oz/¾ cup red wine
175 ml/6 fl oz/¾ cup beef stock

1 Using a sharp knife, cut a pocket deeply into the thickest part of each rib roast for the stuffing.

2 To make the stuffing, melt the butter in a pan, add the chopped onion, green (bell) pepper, celery and garlic and cook until golden, about 10 minutes.

3 Add the thyme, cayenne and breadcrumbs and mix well. Use half of the mixture to stuff each rib roast. Tie the roasts firmly with string, tucking in the bay leaves, to make a neat shape and to enclose the stuffing. Season with salt and pepper.

4 Heat the oil in a large heavy-based frying pan and fry the ribs over a high heat, for 2 minutes on each side. Transfer the ribs with the juices to a roasting pan.

5 Cook in the preheated oven for 15 minutes, turning the meat halfway through, for rare beef. Cook for a further 5-7 minutes for medium beef. Remove from the pan and leave to rest in a warm place while preparing the sauce.

6 Add the flour to the pan juices and cook for 1 minute, stirring constantly, gradually add the wine and stock, bring to the boil and simmer to make a smooth sauce. Serve the ribs with a little of the sauce poured over.

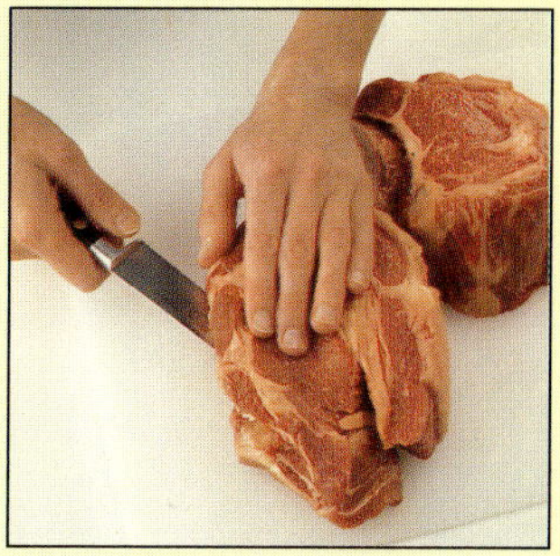
STEP 1

STEP 3a

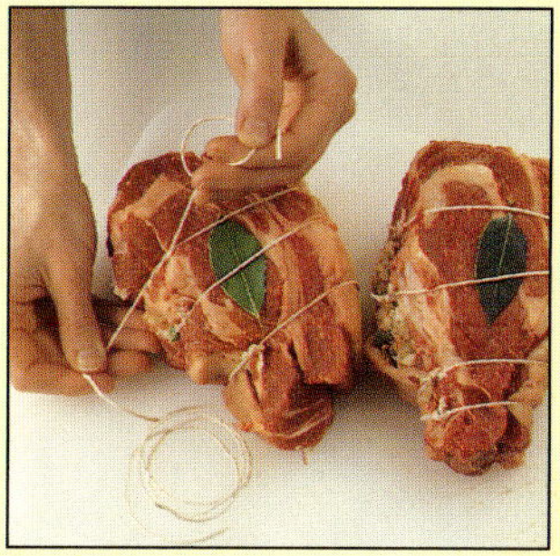
STEP 3b

STEP 4

STEP 1

STEP 3

STEP 4

STEP 5

BEEF DAUBE

Yes, very French but also very, very New Orleans, especially when the beef is perked up with Tabasco and Cajun spices.

SERVES 6-8
OVEN: 160°C/325°F/GAS 3

2 tbsp olive oil
1 large onion, cut into wedges
2 celery sticks, chopped
1 green (bell) pepper, cored, seeded and chopped
1.15 kg/2¼ lb braising steak, cubed
60 g/2 oz/½ cup plain flour, seasoned with salt and pepper
600 ml/1 pint/2½ cups beef stock
2 garlic cloves, crushed
150 ml/¼ pint/⅔ cup red wine
2 tbsp red wine vinegar
2 tbsp tomato purée (paste)
½ tsp Tabasco
1 tsp chopped fresh thyme
2 bay leaves
½ tsp Cajun Spice Mixture (see page 20)
French bread, to serve

1 Heat the oil in a large heavy-based, flameproof casserole. Add the onion wedges and cook until browned on all sides. Remove with a slotted spoon and set aside.

2 Add the celery and (bell) pepper to the pan and cook until softened. Remove the vegetables with a slotted spoon and set aside.

3 Coat the meat in the seasoned flour, add to the pan and sauté until browned on all sides.

4 Add the stock, garlic, wine, vinegar, tomato purée (paste), Tabasco and thyme and heat gently, scraping up any sediment.

5 Return the onions, celery and peppers to the pan. Tuck in the bay leaves and sprinkle with the Cajun seasoning. Bring to the boil, transfer to the oven and cook for 2½-3 hours, or until the meat and vegetables are tender. Serve with French bread.

CAJUN MEATLOAF

Cajun meatloaf is a well-flavoured, rustic affair made with beef, Cajun vegetables and lots of gutsy spices. This is real soul food, to enjoy with rice, seasonal vegetables and a flavoursome Creole sauce.

SERVES 6
OVEN: 180°C/350°F/GAS 4

2 tbsp vegetable oil
1 onion, finely chopped
1 green (bell) pepper, cored, seeded and finely chopped
2 celery sticks, finely chopped
1 garlic clove, crushed
4 tbsp snipped chives
1 kg/2 lb lean minced beef
2 tbsp tomato purée (paste)
2 tsp molasses
1/4 tsp Tabasco
1/2 tsp Worcestershire sauce
1 tsp salt
2 large eggs
60 g/2 oz/1 cup soft white breadcrumbs
Creole Sauce (see page 41)

1 Heat the oil in a large, heavy-based pan, add the onion, green (bell) pepper, celery, garlic and chives, mixing well. Cook over a gentle heat until tender and just beginning to turn golden, about 10-15 minutes.

2 Meanwhile, place the beef in a bowl and break down with a fork. Add the tomato purée (paste), molasses, Tabasco, Worcestershire sauce and salt, mixing well.

3 Add the cooked vegetable mixture, eggs and breadcrumbs and mix well to combine thoroughly.

4 Using wetted hands, shape the mixture into a loaf and place on a baking tray lined with greased foil.

5 Bake for about 1½ hours in the preheated oven until brown and cooked all the way through.

6 Serve hot cut into thick slices with seasonal vegetables and the hot Creole Sauce.

VARIATION

Brush the meatloaf with 2 tablespoons tomato purée (paste) or tomato ketchup before baking to get a really good rich colour, if liked.

STEP 1

STEP 2

STEP 3

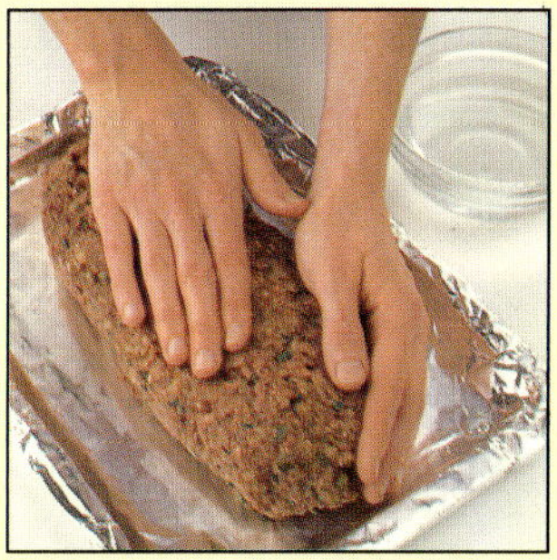

STEP 4

STEP 2

STEP 4

STEP 5a

STEP 5b

PIQUANTE (BELL) PEPPERS

Bell peppers are found in abundance in Cajun and Creole cooking, principally as a flavouring ingredient. Here, they have a starring role, stuffed with savoury rice and baked in a rich tomato sauce.

SERVES 4
OVEN: 180°C/350°/GAS 4

4 large (bell) peppers, red, green or yellow
30 g/1 oz/2 tbsp butter
1 onion, finely chopped
1 large celery stick, finely chopped
150 g/5 oz/1¼ cups cooked long-grain rice
2 tbsp chopped spring onions (scallions)
1 tbsp chopped mixed herbs
250 g/8 oz/1 cup chopped cooked meat, such as ham, chicken or sausage
1 large egg, beaten
salt and pepper

SAUCE:
1 x 425 g/14 oz can chopped tomatoes with herbs
1 garlic clove, crushed
½ tsp Tabasco
1 tsp sugar
1 tsp paprika

1 Cut the tops off the (bell) peppers, then remove the core and seeds.

2 Place the (bell) pepper shells and caps in a saucepan of boiling water and cook for about 6 minutes until softened but not limp. Remove with a slotted spoon and leave to drain upside down while preparing the filling.

3 To make the filling, melt the butter in a heavy-based pan, add the onion and celery and cook until softened. Remove from the heat.

4 Stir in the rice, spring onions (scallions), herbs, meat, egg and salt and pepper to taste, mixing well.

5 Pack the mixture into the par-cooked (bell) pepper shells and replace the par-cooked caps. Place in a baking dish so that the (bell) peppers are packed snugly together.

6 To make the sauce, mix all the ingredients well with salt and pepper to taste and spoon around and between the (bell) peppers. Bake for about 40-45 minutes until tender. Serve hot.

(BELL) PEPPERS

(Bell) peppers now come in a wide variety of colours – orange, yellow, white and black, as well as the usual red and green ones. Look for shiny, unwrinkled ones, and avoid any that have soft spots.

STEP 1a

STEP 1b

STEP 2

STEP 3

VEGETABLES & BOUDIN SAUSAGES

This is a typical dish served at a Cajun Fais Do Do party. The party fun consists of Cajun dancing, lots of eating, friendship, laughter and much merry-making. A party not to be missed!

SERVES 4

15 g/½ oz/1 tbsp butter or margarine
500 g/1 lb Boudin or other spicy sausage
250 g/8 oz bacon or gammon pieces, sliced
2 large onions, chopped
3 celery sticks, chopped
1 red (bell) pepper, cored, seeded and cut into bite-sized pieces
1 green (bell) pepper, cored, seeded and cut into bite-sized pieces
125 g/4 oz okra (optional)
2-3 tsp Cajun Spice Mixture *(see page 20)*
3 tomatoes, skinned and chopped
300 ml/½ pt/1¼ cups chicken stock
chopped parsley, to garnish

1 Cut the sausages into bite-sized pieces. Melt the butter in a large, heavy-based pan. Add the bacon or gammon followed by the sausages and cook quickly until browned on all sides. Remove from the pan with a slotted spoon and set aside.

2 Add the onions, celery, (bell) peppers and okra to the pan and sauté until softened.

3 Add the spice mixture to the pan, stirring well. Cook for 5 minutes over low heat.

4 Add the tomatoes and stock, mixing well.

5 Return the bacon pieces and sausages to the pan. Cover and simmer for about 35 minutes until cooked. Serve with rice.

BOUDIN SAUSAGES

These are spicy, open-textured sausages made from pork, rice, pork liver and seasonings and are well worth seeking out. If you can't find them use any other spicy sausage instead.

CHAPTER FOUR

Accompaniments

Cajun-Creole cuisine can be homely and rustic on the one hand and original and flamboyant on the other. Most of the recipes in this section come from the former camp, and were originally intended to eke out meagre supplies or expensive prime foods. That is not to say they are just "fillers", for each dish now has its own status, and band of enthusiastic devotees.

Cornbread and its cousin spoonbread, for example, are golden squares or scoops of pure nourishment, being made from cornmeal (polenta), eggs, milk and butter. They are delicious served at breakfast-time with butter, or at a main meal with foods like fried chicken. Native American Maque Choux is a colourful array of sun-soaked corn kernels with onion, green (bell) pepper, tomato and spices that is best eaten as a delicious side dish to roasts and grills; while Hush Puppies are marvellous mouth-watering fritters made with flavoured cornmeal, all the better for serving with fried fish.

Don't miss out by skipping on the sampling of such interesting extras. They give a meal an indefinable Cajun authenticity that no main dish alone can sustain.

Opposite: *A jester at the Mardi Gras celebrations in New Orleans.*

STEP 1

STEP 3

STEP 4

STEP 5

HUSH PUPPIES

Legend has it that these were thrown to hungry and noisy hunting dogs when they returned home with their masters after a day's hunting, so that a little peace could be enjoyed – hence the name.

MAKES ABOUT 24

150 g/5 oz/1 cup cornmeal
60 g/2 oz/½ cup self-raising flour
2 tbsp cornflour (cornstarch)
1 tbsp baking powder
1 tsp Cajun Spice Mixture (see page 20)
¼ tsp chilli powder
1 garlic clove, crushed
2 tbsp grated onion
2 eggs, beaten
175 ml/6 fl oz/¾ cup milk
vegetable oil, for deep frying

1 Mix the cornmeal with the flour, cornflour (cornstarch), baking powder, spice mixture and chilli powder.

2 Mix the garlic with the onion and eggs and stir into the flour mixture.

3 Heat the milk until hot but not boiling then pour over the cornmeal mixture and stir well to mix. Allow to cool.

4 Heat the oil in a large, heavy-based pan until hot. Carefully add about 5 heaped teaspoonfuls of the mixture to the oil and deep-fry until puffy and a light golden colour, about 1 minute, turning over occasionally.

5 Remove with a slotted spoon and drain on paper towels. Keep warm.

6 Repeat with the remaining mixture, cooking about 5 hush puppies at a time, for best results. Serve immediately, as an accompaniment to fried fish fillets.

VARIATION

These fried cornmeal fritters are crisp and golden on the outside and mellow, soft and fluffy on the inside. These are traditionally served with fried fish, but are also good as finger fare with drinks. To be really Southern, the Hush Puppies should be fried in the pan after the fish has been fried, using the same fat or oil.

NATIVE AMERICAN MAQUE CHOUX

This classic corn dish was introduced to the Cajuns by the local Native Americans. It is stepped up in flavour with traditional Cajun ingredients: onion, green (bell) pepper, tomato and Tabasco sauce.

STEP 1

STEP 2

STEP 3

STEP 4

SERVES 4-6

1 large tomato
15 g/½ oz/1 tbsp butter or margarine
½ onion, chopped
1 small green (bell) pepper, cored, seeded and chopped
750 g/1½ lb/generous 4 cups sweetcorn kernels, defrosted if frozen
½ tsp salt
½ tsp Tabasco sauce

1 Skin, seed and roughly chop the tomato.

2 Melt the butter or margarine in a large heavy-based pan. Add the onion and (bell) pepper and cook for 5 minutes until tender.

3 Stir in the corn, tomato, salt and Tabasco, stirring well.

4 Reduce the heat to a gentle simmer and cook the mixture for 10-15 minutes or until the corn is tender.

5 Serve hot with meat, poultry, rice and pasta dishes.

TABASCO

Tabasco is an essential ingredient in Cajun-Creole cooking. The sauce is made with red chilli pepper, vinegar and salt. It was first manufactured in Louisiana in the 19th century and is now the world's best-known pepper sauce.

FRESH CORN

Fresh corn kernels undoubtedly make the best Maque Choux. To remove the kernels from fresh cobs, pull away the leaves and all the silks clinging to the corn, then trim the stems level with the base of the cobs. Stand each cob upright, pointed end uppermost, then slice away the kernels with a sharp knife as close to the cob as possible. Fresh corn kernels can be frozen for up to 12 months for convenience.

STEP 1

STEP 2

STEP 3

STEP 4

RED BEANS 'N' RICE

This slow-cooked red kidney bean and vegetable mixture was traditionally made and served on Monday. It would be left simmering on the stove while the women washed clothes in the Mississippi river.

SERVES 4

175 g/6 oz streaky bacon, rinded and chopped
1 large onion, chopped
2 celery sticks, chopped
1 green (bell) pepper, cored and chopped
2 garlic cloves, crushed
½ tsp ground bay leaves
dash of Tabasco
2 tbsp tomato purée (paste)
4 tsp chopped parsley
1 x 475 g/15 oz can red kidney beans, undrained
salt and pepper
boiled rice, to serve

1 Place the bacon in a pan over a gentle heat and cook until the fat starts to run.

2 Add the onion, celery, (bell) pepper and garlic and mix well. Cover and cook gently for about 15 minutes or until well softened.

3 Add the bay leaves, Tabasco, tomato purée (paste), parsley, kidney beans and salt and pepper to taste. Stir well to mix.

4 Cover the pan and simmer for a further 30 minutes, stirring occasionally.

5 Serve hot with freshly cooked rice for a main meal, or as an accompaniment to a meat dish.

ALTERNATIVE

Some of the bacon may be replaced with smoked pork sausage if liked. Reduce the amount of bacon to 60 g/2 oz and add 1 tablespoon of oil to cook the vegetables, then add 125 g/4 oz thickly sliced smoked pork sausage with the beans.

CORNBREAD

This is a lovely, golden bread that is best served with butter while still warm. Use any stale bread to make stuffings or toppings for gratin-style dishes.

MAKES 1 LOAF
OVEN: 180°C/350°F/GAS 4

175 g/6 oz/1½ cups self-raising flour
150 g/5 oz/1 cup fine cornmeal
30 g/1 oz/¼ cup cornflour (cornstarch)
pinch of salt
1 tsp baking powder
60 g/2 oz/¼ cup caster sugar
350 ml/12 fl oz/1½ cups milk
90 g/3 oz/6 tbsp butter
1 egg, beaten

1 Place a 30 x 20 cm/12 x 8 in shallow oblong baking tin in the preheated oven for 5 minutes.

2 To make the cornbread, mix the flour in a bowl with the cornmeal, cornflour (cornstarch), salt, baking powder and sugar.

3 Warm the milk in a small pan with 60 g/2 oz/¼ cup of the butter until it is slightly hot and the butter has melted. Remove the milk and butter mixture from the heat and beat in the egg. Melt the remaining butter and set aside.

4 Stir the milk and egg mixture into the flour mixture and mix well.

5 Remove the hot tin from the oven, brush with butter to grease then pour in the batter. Smooth the top to level the mixture.

6 Bake in the oven for 25 minutes, remove from the oven, brush with the melted butter and cook for a further 15 minutes until golden and firm to the touch. Serve hot, cut into squares.

SERVING

Cornbread is traditionally served with butter for breakfast or eaten with main dishes like fried chicken or fish, as a side dish.

STEP 2

STEP 3

STEP 4

STEP 5

CHAPTER FIVE

Puddings

Cajun and Creole desserts are not only heavenly to taste; they have wonderful names that conjure up a colourful tapestry of the area: Belle of the South Pecan Tart, Ambrosia and Mississippi Mud Pie. Many should be savoured slowly, like a long journey on a paddleboat steamer up the Mississippi, because they are wickedly rich and truly indulgent.

Again, many have a colourful cast of ingredients. Bread Pudding is made with humble French bread, dried fruit and warm exotic spices then served with a whiskey or bourbon sauce; Pecan Tart is made with the rich crop of pecan nuts and literally drools with golden syrup over its crisp French pastry crust; Ambrosia, meanwhile, is the dessert that is served at Christmas, or for the Mardi Gras gods, since it is a heavenly combination of home-grown sharp orange and pineapple pieces with sweet preserved cherries and coconut.

No selection would be complete without the world-renowned Mississippi Mud Pie, named after the so-called bayous of Louisiana. This chocoholic's delight cries out to be sampled. Dig through the layers of fluffy meringue, silky smooth ice-cream, then crisp pastry for an unforgettable experience. You may think you have discovered heaven!

Opposite: *"Oak Alley", one of the stately plantation houses on the Mississippi, a reminder of the South's past.*

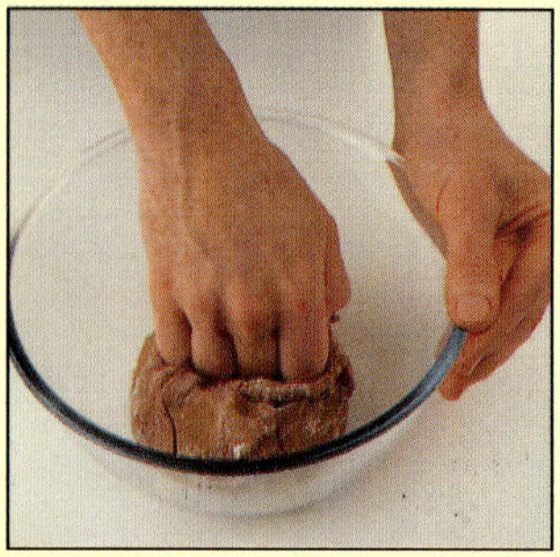

STEP 1a

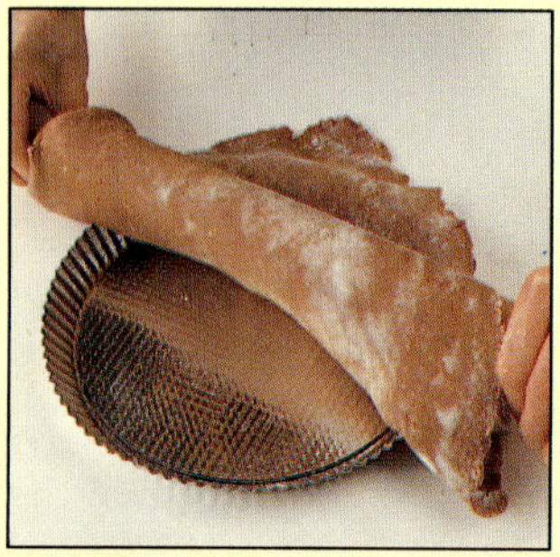

STEP 1b

STEP 4

STEP 5

MISSISSIPPI MUD PIE

Mississippi Mud Pie, named after the Bayou areas in Louisiana, is a devilishly good dessert of flavoured ice-cream frozen in a pastry tart crowned with a fluffy hat of meringue – somewhat like a Baked Alaska. .

SERVES 6-8
OVEN: 200°C/400°F/GAS 6;
THEN 230°C/450°F/GAS 8

PASTRY:
250 g/8 oz/2 cups plain flour
125 g/4 oz/½ cup butter, softened
30 g/1 oz/2 tbsp caster sugar
1 tbsp cocoa powder, sifted (optional)
4-5 tbsp iced water

FILLING:
½ recipe Creole Ice-cream (page 67)
½ recipe Chocolate Creole Ice-cream (page 67)

TOPPING:
3 egg whites
175 g/6 oz/¾ cup caster sugar

1 To make the pastry, sift the flour into a bowl, then rub in the butter until the mixture resembles fine breadcrumbs. Stir in the sugar and cocoa powder, if using (to make a chocolate-flavoured pie crust), until well mixed. Add the water and mix to a firm but pliable dough. Roll out the pastry thinly. Grease a 23 cm/9 in loose-bottomed fluted flan tin or dish and line with the pastry. Trim off surplus pastry level with the top of the tin.

2 Bake "blind" in the preheated oven for 25 minutes. Remove the paper and beans and bake for a further 10-15 minutes or until crisp and golden. Remove from the oven and allow to cool completely.

3 About 15 minutes before required, remove the ice-creams from the freezer and allow to soften slightly.

4 Scoop the ice-creams into the pastry case then return to the freezer to freeze while making the meringue topping.

5 To make the topping, whisk the egg whites until they stand in firm peaks. Gradually whisk in the sugar, 1 tablespoon at a time, until the meringue is very thick and glossy. Swirl or pipe over the frozen ice-cream mixture to completely enclose.

6 Bake in the oven for about 5 minutes or until the meringue is tinged golden. Serve the pie at once, cut into wedges.

CREOLE ICE-CREAM

Creole ice-cream is made with crème fraîche, now widely available in supermarkets. It has a rich, if slightly sour, flavour that is perfect for ices.

SERVES 6

200 g/7 oz/generous cup crème fraîche
600 ml/1 pint/2½ cups custard, lightly sweetened to taste
few drops of vanilla essence
90 g/3 oz/6 tbsp caster sugar

1 Mix the crème fraîche with the custard, vanilla essence to taste and caster sugar, mixing well.

2 Pour into a freezer-proof container and place in the freezer or freezing compartment of the refrigerator. Freeze until almost firm.

3 Remove the ice-cream from the freezer and beat or whisk until smooth – this helps to break down the large ice crystals that form and will keep the ice-cream smooth and creamy.

4 Return to the freezer and freeze until firm, about 2 hours.

5 Remove the ice-cream from the freezer about 15 minutes before serving to soften slightly – this will make scooping or slicing easier.

6 Scoop or slice into chilled glasses and serve at once .

VARIATIONS

CHOCOLATE CREOLE ICE-CREAM: Prepare as above but add 125 g/4 oz/4 squares melted plain chocolate to the basic mixture.

CREOLE FUDGE ICE-CREAM: Prepare as above but add 250 g/8 oz fudge that has been gently melted over a low heat with 3 tablespoons milk.

STEP 1

STEP 2

STEP 3

STEP 5

STEP 1

STEP 3

STEP 4

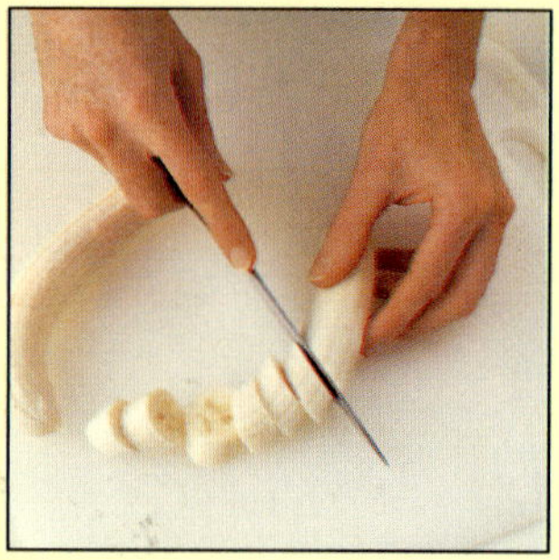

STEP 5

AMBROSIA

Ambrosia is food fit for the Mardi Gras Gods! A delicious concoction of fruits and coconut that is all the better for serving with a generous spoonful of soured cream or crème fraîche.

SERVES 6

1 pineapple
6 oranges
125 g/4 oz/¾ cup maraschino cherries
60 g/2 oz/⅔ cup desiccated (shredded) coconut
2 bananas (optional)
soured cream or crème fraîche, to serve

1 Peel and core the pineapple then cut the flesh into bite-sized pieces. Place in a mixing bowl.

2 Peel the oranges, remove the pith then segment the flesh. Add to the pineapple.

3 Thoroughly drain the cherries and add to the fruit mixture, mixing well.

4 Stir in the coconut, cover and chill for at least 8 hours or overnight.

5 Just before serving, peel and thinly slice the bananas (if used). Stir into the fruit and coconut mixture.

6 Serve the fruit in individual bowls topped with a dollop of the soured cream or crème fraîche.

CREME FRAICHE

With its delicious tangy flavour, crème fraîche adds another dimension of richness to sauces and desserts. It can be made at home by combining 150 ml/¼ pint/⅔ cup double (heavy) cream with 1 tbsp buttermilk in a small stainless steel or glass bowl. Cover and keep in a warm place overnight. The crème fraîche should have thickened to the consistency of warm yogurt. Refrigerate for up to 1 week.

AMBROSIA

This is a very old, traditional US recipe and many variations exist. Maraschino cherries are a fairly modern addition, but they add a splash of colour to the dish.

STEP 1a

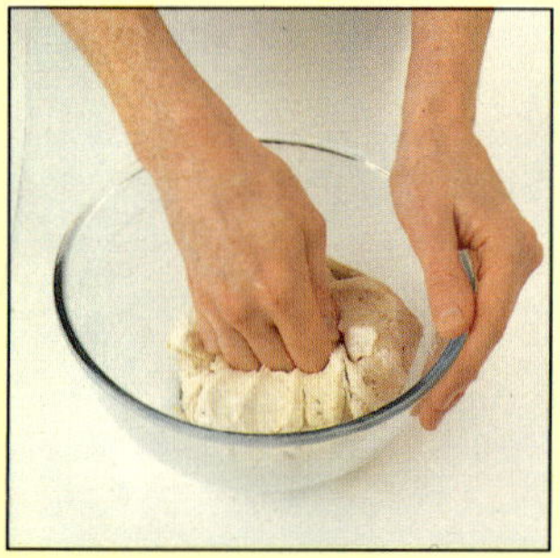

STEP 1b

STEP 3

STEP 4

BELLE OF THE SOUTH PECAN TART

A beauty of a pie not unlike treacle tart. Serve with lashings of softly whipped cream and watch the men drool!

SERVES 8-10
OVEN: 190°C/375°F/GAS 5

PASTRY:
250 g/8 oz/2 cups plain flour
125 g/4 oz/½ cup butter, softened
2 tbsp finely chopped pecans (optional)
4-5 tbsp iced water

FILLING:
200 g/7 oz/1 cup pecans
3 large eggs, beaten
250 g/8 oz/1 cup caster sugar
250 g/8 oz/¾ cup golden syrup
30 g/1 oz/2 tbsp butter, melted
1 tsp vanilla essence
whipped cream, to serve

1 To make the pastry, sift the flour into a bowl, then rub in the butter until the mixture resembles fine breadcrumbs. Stir in the chopped pecans, if using, then the water, and mix to a firm but pliable dough.

2 Roll out the pastry thinly. Grease a 25 cm/10 in fluted flan tin or dish and line with the pastry. Trim off the surplus pastry from the edge.

3 Sprinkle the pecans evenly over the base of the tart.

4 To make the filling, beat the eggs with the sugar, golden syrup, butter and vanilla essence, mixing well. Pour or spoon over the pecans.

5 Bake in the preheated oven for about 45 minutes or until the pastry is crisp and golden and the filling is firm.

6 Allow to cool slightly before cutting into wedges. Serve with softly whipped cream.

PECANS

Pecan nuts grow in profusion in the South – it is a wild tree native to the US. Pecan nuts are now widely available, though if they are unobtainable walnuts can also be used.

STEP 1

STEP 2a

STEP 2b

STEP 4

COCONUT PIE

This sweet pie is frequently served at special gatherings, where no matter what the occasion, from weddings to funerals, the object is to celebrate with rich sweet pickings.

SERVES **8-10**
OVEN: 200°C/400°/GAS 6
THEN 180°C/350°F/GAS 4

PASTRY:
250 g/8 oz/2 cups plain flour
125 g/4 oz/½ cup butter, softened
2 tbsp desiccated (shredded) coconut
4-5 tbsp iced water

FILLING:
5 large eggs, beaten
150 g/5 oz/1⅔ cups desiccated (shredded) coconut
350 g/12 oz/1½ cups caster sugar
125 g/4 oz/½ cup butter, melted
150 ml/¼ pint/⅔ cup buttermilk or 4 tbsp natural yogurt mixed with 4 tbsp skimmed milk
1 tsp vanilla essence

1 To make the pastry, sift the flour into a bowl, then rub in the butter in pieces until the mixture resembles fine breadcrumbs. Stir in the coconut and water and mix to a firm but pliable dough.

2 Roll out the pastry thinly and use to line a 25 cm/10 in greased fluted flan tin or dish. Bake "blind" in the preheated oven for 25 minutes. Remove the paper and beans and bake for a further 10-15 minutes or until crisp and golden. Remove from the oven then reduce the oven temperature.

3 To make the filling, beat the eggs with the coconut, sugar, butter, buttermilk and vanilla, mixing well.

4 Pour into the baked pastry case. Return to the oven and cook for about 45 minutes or until the filling has set and is firm to the touch.

5 Turn off the heat and leave the pie to stand in the oven, with the door open, for a further 15 minutes.

6 Serve warm or when just cold, but not chilled.

VARIATIONS

There are many variations of the coconut pie, a favourite in the South. In some versions the pastry case is filled with a sweet coconut custard and allowed to set. When cold the top is sprinkled with toasted coconut and decorated with whipped cream.

BOURBON WHISKEY
PRODUCT OF USA
40% Vol

BREAD PUDDING WITH BOURBON

This crusty, golden-crowned pudding is made in a trice. The authentic crowning glory is, of course, the bourbon sauce!

STEP 1

SERVES 6
OVEN: 180°C/350°F/GAS 4

100 g/3½ oz stale French bread, broken into pieces
300 ml/½ pint/1¼ cups milk or half milk and half double (heavy) cream
125 g/4 oz/½ cup sugar
45 g/1½ oz/3 tbsp butter, melted
1 egg, lightly beaten
60 g/2 oz/⅓ cup raisins
30 g/1 oz/⅓ cup desiccated (shredded) coconut
45 g/1½ oz/⅓ cup chopped pecans
¼ tsp ground cinnamon
large pinch grated nutmeg

BOURBON SAUCE:
60 g/2 oz/¼ cup butter
90 g/3 oz/⅔ cup icing (confectioner's) sugar
1 small egg yolk (size 4)
50 ml/2 fl oz/¼ cup Bourbon

1 To make the pudding, mix all the ingredients together in a large mixing bowl – the mixture should be very moist but not soupy.

2 Pour the pudding mixture into a buttered 900 ml/1½ pint/3½ cup baking dish.

3 Bake in the middle of the preheated oven for about 45 minutes or until the pudding is set and the top is a dark golden colour.

4 Meanwhile, to make the sauce, cream the butter with the sugar in a small saucepan over a gentle heat until all the butter has been absorbed.

5 Remove from the heat and blend in the egg yolk. Gradually beat in the Bourbon. Serve warm poured over the pudding – the sauce thickens as it cools.

STEP 2

STEP 3

STEP 5

ALTERNATIVE

Malt whisky can be used instead of Bourbon if liked.

CAJUN & CREOLE COOKING

CAJUN SEASONING

This is a combination of the main herbs and seasonings used in Cajun-Creole cooking. The spices should be mixed together and stored in a screw-topped jar. Cajun seasoning mix can be bought ready-made from specialist shops but here is a recipe for a good home-made one

1 tbsp garlic powder or salt
1 tbsp onion powder or onion salt
2 tsp ground white pepper
2 tsp ground black pepper
1½ tsp cayenne pepper
2 tsp dried thyme
½ tsp dried oregano
pinch of dried cumin
pinch of dried basil

Cajun and Creole cuisines originated in Louisiana. These cooking styles are a melting pot of varied cultures, among them Native American, French, Spanish and African. They evolved as each new ethnic group combined the best of its own traditions with ingredients that were available locally. Tradition has it that Cajun cuisine was for poor folk and Creole for aristocrats.

Another way to describe the difference between Creole and Cajun food is to explain that a Creole would use ten chickens in a dish for one person, whilst a Cajun would use one chicken to feed ten people. That is not to say that Cajuns are mean. Far from it. They are generous, warm-hearted people. However, traditionally they were poor, southern Louisiana country folk, very unlike their rich, privileged, New Orleans city dwelling cousins.

Creole food is therefore the sophisticated city food of New Orleans, based on the French culinary traditions appplied to local delicacies, and Cajun is the cookery of the rugged people who then lived in the bayous – the waterways and swamps that dot Louisiana. These people lived off the land, being mostly trappers and fishermen, and cooked their daily catch in a big black iron pot over an open fire. It was, and still is, hearty, robust cookery.

Over the centuries, the difference between Cajuns and Creoles evened out and today they live harmoniously together on equal terms, sharing food, music, culture and hospitality.

Cajun cuisine relies on what can be grown or hunted in the immediate locality. That is why it makes such good use of locally grown rice, seafood, freshwater fish from the bayous (rivers) and wild or farmed hogs and pigs. The Cajuns love their food spicy and most dishes are pepped up to the required standards with Tabasco sauce and Cajun Spice Mix (see page 20).

Many of the names of foods, recipes and traditions are in a form of pure or adapted French. This is because the Cajuns were originally from southern France. A number of French emigrated to Nova Scotia at the beginning of the 17th century and founded a colony which they named Acadia. Unfortunately, due to religious persecution the settlers were driven out and forced to seek a new home. Eventually the Cajuns arrived in southern Louisiana where they settled and can be found today still speaking their adapted mother tongue. The name Cajun evolved from Acadian. Music plays an important part in their life and today's Cajun bands still produce the traditional distinctive sound heard by their ancestors.

Today, Louisiana is an old traditional world nestling comfortably inside a newer more vibrant one. It is a foot-tapping, hand-clapping, song-humming kind of place where jazz still beats out its soul some 24 hours a day. The jewel in its crown is New Orleans – famed and feted for its fine restaurants, cocktail bars, showy festivals and markets that boast the very finest in succulent seafood, exotic vegetables, fine patissserie and more. Intermingling with this fine culture is more than a hint of the best of Southern country style or Cajun cuisine. This is a marriage of cultures and cuisines made in heaven!

CAJUN AND CREOLE BASICS

Cooking terms, ingredients and other Cajun-Creole essentials:

Blackened This is not a traditional Cajun cooking technique but one invented by the famous New Orleans chef, Paul Prudhomme. A prime piece of meat, poultry or fish is coated in a spice and herb mixture then cooked quickly in a white hot, smoking cast-iron pan. The intense heat creates a blackened exterior whilst the flesh inside stays moist.

Boudin A spicy, open-textured sausage made from rice, pork, pork liver, onion and seasonings. When hard to find use any other spicy, coarse-textured sausage.

Bread Pudding A favourite Cajun dessert not unlike our own but served with a hot, whisky or bourbon sauce.

Cajun Popcorn These are prawns that have been sprinkled with Cajun seasoning then coated in batter and deep fried. They are eaten in New Orleans as a hot snack or starter with a remoulade dipping sauce.

Cayenne Pepper Pepper made from a type of chilli pepper that is cooked with flour then dried and finely ground for use in dishes that need a "kick".

Crawfish Or crayfish, these are crustaceans which look like small lobsters. Only the tail meat is eaten. Lobster, scampi or large green prawns can be used instead.

Etouffé This is a term that means smothered and refers to a dish that is smothered with plenty of sauce.

Fish Stock Many Cajun-Creole fish or seafood dishes require fish stock. This is easiest made by simmering fish bones and heads in water for about 15-20 minutes, then straining for use. Alternatively, canned seafood bisque of the condensed variety will also make an excellent alternative.

Grillades Pronounced "gree-ards", these are served at breakfast or brunch. Basically they are slices of beef or veal in thick gravy. Traditionally, they are always served with a sort of cornmeal porridge called grits.

Grits Hominy grits are a creamy white cereal that looks like coarse semolina, made from corn with the husks removed. You can find it in specialist stores but cooked couscous makes a good, if not authentic, alternative.

Gumbo A hearty, rich, thick soup, almost a stew. It is made by combining any variety of poultry, seafood and spiced sausage, with Tabasco sauce. Cajuns enjoy arguing over whether it should be

CYCLONE COCKTAIL

Get your dinner party off to a good start by serving a Cajun-style cocktail before the meal. Cyclone is a wonderful concoction, with just the right amount of kick to help break the ice.

Serves 1

50 ml/2 fl oz vodka
25 ml/1 fl oz passion fruit or mango juice
25 ml/1 fl oz fresh lemon juice
crushed ice

1. Shake the vodka with the fruit juices until well blended. Half-fill a glass with crushed ice.

2. Pour the cocktail into the glass and decorate lavishly with fruit and citrus leaves.

SHRIMP REMOULADE

If you've one eye on the clock and an instant starter to make, this Southern version of the prawn cocktail is the answer.

SERVES 6

4 tbsp vegetable oil
2 tbsp red wine vinegar
2 tbsp mustard, or to taste
2 tsp horseradish
dash of Tabasco
1 tsp ground paprika
2 tbsp chopped parsley
$^1/_2$ bunch spring onions (scallions), chopped
750 g/ 1$^1/_2$ lb peeled prawns (shrimp)
salad leaves, to serve

1. Beat the oil with the vinegar, mustard, horseradish sauce, Tabasco and paprika until well mixed.

2. Stir in the parsley, onions and prawns (shrimp). Chill thoroughly and serve over salad leaves.

thickened with filé or okra. The name gumbo is thought to derive from a similar African word meaning okra. Gumbo is always served with hot cooked rice.

Gumbo Filé Filé is sassafras leaves ground to a fine powder which is used to thicken gumbos. It is added prior to serving rather than during cooking because it turns stringy when cooked. Very hard to find outside the USA.

Hush Puppies Fried cornmeal fritters that are generally served with fried fish.

Jambalaya A spicy rice dish, usually made with several types of meat and traditionally almost always with the highly seasoned smoked ham known as tasso. Tasso is virtually unobtainable outside Louisiana. A good home-made substitute can be made by coating smoked gammon cubes in Cajun seasoning mix.

Maque Choux This is a corn dish made with sweetcorn, (bell) peppers, onion and tomato and was introduced to the Cajuns by the local Red Indians.

Mirlitons These are pear-shaped vegetables from the same family as the marrow or squash that are traditionally stuffed and also used in sweet and savoury dishes. They are also known as chayote or christophene.

Po-Boys Short for poor boy. These are hearty sandwiches made on French bread. In days gone by these were considered the cheapest lunch possible – they were just a huge sandwich filled fit-to-burst with anything from the usual ham and cheese to meatballs, fried chicken or fried oysters. They have always been consumed by rich and poor alike but are not so cheap to purchase in Louisiana today.

Pralines Pralines are a cross between a sweet and a cookie and have the texture of softish fudge. They are usually very sweet and crammed with pecans. They are generally served with tea alongside other cakes or after a meal with coffee like mints.

Red Beans 'N' Rice A hearty mixture of red kidney beans and rice, flavoured traditionally with pickled pork or ham hock, bay leaves and Tabasco. It is slow-cooked and traditionally served on a Monday. It would be left simmering on the stove whilst the women washed clothes in the Mississippi river.

Redfish This is the favourite fish for blackening. The flesh is mild and sweet and the fish has a black spot on the tail. Many fishmongers now stock redfish fillets but when unavailable you can use red snapper, salmon or haddock fillets instead.

Remoulade Sauce A sauce made from mayonnaise, hot Creole mustard and Tabasco sauce. It is used as a dip for shrimp or as a salad dressing.

Roux A roux is one of the most important mixtures required in Cajun-Creole cooking. It is a mixture of flour and oil that is cooked slowly, sometimes for hours to produce a deeply-coloured paste which gives a characteristic nutty, toasty flavour to the finished dish. A roux is also required to thicken the juices of a dish. As a general rule, the darker the roux the less its thickening ability. The Cajuns prepare a light, medium or dark roux depending upon whether it is to be used for thickening or flavour.

Sauce Piquante A tomato sauce, served hot and spiced very liberally with Tabasco sauce.

Soft Shell Crabs These are small crabs that are caught after they moult and before they can grow their new shells. They are sautéed in butter or deep-fried in batter for eating.

Tabasco Sauce This is the Cajun-Creole cooking essential. A true Cajun cannot tolerate bland food. Tabasco sauce is a combination of red pepper (called Tabasco pepper), vinegar and salt. It is made by the McIlhenny family at their home on Avery Island, Louisiana. Originally Edmund McIlhenny, who created the sauce in 1868, made it for his family and close friends but it proved so popular that he began to sell it to local people. News of this unique sauce quickly spread, and now Tabasco is the world's best known pepper sauce.

The Trinity Also called the holy trinity, it is a combination of onion, green peppers and celery. The Trinity is essential to Cajun cuisine and appears in virtually every recipe.

CAJUN AND CREOLE FESTIVALS

Cajuns love to party so it is not surprising that their favourite saying is *laissez les bon temps roulez* (let the good times roll). To this end they have devised a number of party and festival occasions, a few of which are described below:

Boucherie Before refrigeration there was no way of preserving slaughtered livestock for future use. Therefore, the whole animal had to be cooked or preserved immediately to avoid waste. The boucherie came around once a month. Everyone would gather together, the men would butcher and clean and the women would prepare tasso, boudin, sausage and hogshead cheese. Following a long day's work the event would become a celebration.

Couchon de Lait This a dining festival and involved the slaughtering of a suckling pig which was then cooked over a slow fire until crispy and tender.

Crayfish Boil This is a serious outdoor eating party. Enormous quantities of crayfish are boiled in enormous tubs over an open fire. Guests sit around and simply eat and talk until they disappear from view under a pile of shells!

Fais Do Do This is the ultimate good time party. Translated, it means time for babies and young children to sleep while the adults have fun. The fun consists of dancing to a Cajun band, lots of eating, drinking, laughter and much merry-making.

CREME FRAICHE

This French cream is delicious with Cajun and Creole desserts and is used for making Creole ice-cream. It can now be found in many supermarkets. If you have trouble finding it the following is a good alternative.

Mix equal quantities of soured and double (heavy) cream together and whisk gently. Cover and leave to stand, without chilling, for 6-10 hours. The mixture is ready when it has slightly thickened and developed a slightly acidic or lactic taste. Chill, and use within one week.

INDEX